For Mum & Dad

the *Rise and Fall* *of* Oscar the Magician

A MONKEY WORLD ADVENTURE

MATTHEW PORTER

little bigfoot
an imprint of sasquatch books
seattle, wa

Oscar the magician received some good news—a nomination from the readers of *Magic Monthly* magazine for the title of Magician of the Year!

"How marvelous!" he said, "and it comes with a lovely big trophy!"

Then Milton read that Oscar the magician would be his competition. Confidence turned quickly to doubt. Milton was good, but could Oscar be better?

"I know: I'll cheat. That's it! I can't lose the trophy! I'll mess up his tricks and make him the fool. Then I'll have the full set of trophies and be written into history as the World's Greatest Magician!"

He consulted a fortune-teller just to make sure.

"I see you bathed in bright light and it looks like you're giving a speech, an acceptance speech perhaps? You're holding a cup, or maybe a trophy? The image is fading. That's all I see."

So Milton the Magnificent, disguised as a janitor, snuck backstage to tamper with a few of Oscar's magic tricks.

During the show, Oscar was chased by a swarm of bees.

The audience, thinking this was part of the act, loved it! They hooted and hollered for more.

Milton tried to break Oscar's magic wand but he only managed to bend it a bit.

Oscar accidentally levitated half the crowd at his next performance. And they loved it!

"What an act!," they said, demanding an encore.

But events took a more serious turn when Oscar's tightrope mysteriously snapped at an outdoor show.

Luckily he landed in a tank of live crabs being driven to a seafood market.

Once again, everybody loved it!

"What a twist! Such impeccable timing!"

Every act of sabotage by Milton only improved Oscar's performance and increased his popularity.

"When I realized they were bees and not ping pong balls, I was a little bit surprised. But you have to roll with the punches in this game. You know what I mean?"

Milton the Magnificent began to worry.

"I'll have to ruin his act in person to be sure he ends up looking the fool."

But things didn't quite go according to plan
and it was Milton who looked the fool.

Oscar's popularity soared just as the voting began.

Thinking he was rehearsing a new routine, Oscar became befuddled by Milton's mysterious monocle.

Under the monocle's spell, Oscar the magician stole the priceless Blue Diamond Necklace from the city museum.

The next morning, he caught the Thunderbolt Express
to meet Milton at his apartment in Miggleswick.

But due to some trouble
with a missing bridge,
Oscar didn't make it to
Milton's apartment.

Instead, he returned to his senses on
top of a box surrounded by jazz-playing
crocodiles.

"Crocodiles! Jazz-playing crocodiles!
How odd!"

Mayday the detective soon arrived at the scene along with police officers Charlie and Joe. They arrested Oscar on suspicion of robbery.

"Oscar the magician, I am arresting you for the theft of the Blue Diamond Necklace!"

In his cold and lonely prison cell, Oscar told Mayday the little he remembered and begged him to look deeper into the case.

"I was rehearsing with Milton, then everything went foggy. I felt really sleepy and woke up by the river. I don't remember doing anything wrong," he sobbed.

Mayday was intrigued and decided to investigate further.

Mayday looked like he was sleepwalking as he made his way up the steps of the city museum.

BLUE DIAMOND EXHIBI

BLUE DIAMOND EXHIBITION
REOPENING
PARTY
BY INVITE ONLY

During the reopening party, Mayday stole the Blue Diamond Necklace, and all the guests were too stunned to catch him.

With the diamond hidden
under his hat, Mayday climbed
on a bus heading for the train
station, closely followed by
Charlie and Joe.

He rode the Thunderbolt
Express to the end of the
line at Miggleswick station.

Milton was in the bath when Mayday burst in and handed over the Blue Diamond Necklace. The monocle had done its job but it didn't win Milton the trophy.

Milton the Magnificent enjoyed confessing and talked like he was collecting a prize. He said, "Only the World's Greatest Magician could pull off such an ingenious crime!"

So Oscar the magician was proven innocent. And *Magic Monthly* magazine named him Magician of the Year.

To celebrate the good news, Oscar threw a rock 'n' roll party with the help of some newfound friends!

Manufactured in China by C&C Offset Printing Co. Ltd.
Shenzhen, Guangdong Province,
in March 2015

Published by Little Bigfoot,
an imprint of Sasquatch Books

20 19 18 18 17 16 15   9 8 7 6 5 4 3 2 1

Editor: Gary Luke
Project editor: Nancy W. Cortelyou
Design: Anna Goldstein
Illustrations: Matthew Porter

Library of Congress Cataloging-in-
Publication Data is available.

ISBN: 978-1-57061-929-8

www.MatthewPorterArt.com

Sasquatch Books
1904 Third Avenue, Suite 710
Seattle, WA 98101
(206) 467-4300
www.sasquatchbooks.com
custserv@sasquatchbooks.com